The Backyard Time Detectives

written and created by
David Suzuki

art by Eugenie Fernandes

Stoddart

Text copyright © 1995 by David Suzuki
Illustrations copyright © 1995 by Eugenie Fernandes

First published in 1995 by
Stoddart Publishing Co. Limited
34 Lesmill Road
Toronto, Canada
M3B 2T6
(416) 445-3333

In the United States contact
Stoddart Publishing Co. Limited
85 River Rock Drive, Unit 202,
Buffalo, New York 14207, 1-800-805-1083

Canadian Cataloguing in Publication Data

Suzuki, David, 1936–
The backyard time detectives

(Nature all around)
ISBN 0-7737-5740-6

1. Natural history – Juvenile literature.
I. Fernandes, Eugenie, 1943–   .   II. Title
III. Series

QH48.S89 1995   j508   C95-930886-5

Editing: Jennifer Glossop
Cover design: Brant Cowie/Art Plus Limited
Computer typesetting: Tannice Goddard/S.O. Networking

Printed in Canada on recycled paper

Stoddart Publishing gratefully acknowledges the support of the Canada
Council, Ontario Ministry of Culture, Tourism and Recreation,
Ontario Arts Council, and Ontario Publishing Centre in the development
of writing and publishing in Canada.

"Come on! Mom and Dad are going to plant the garden," Megan called to her brother. "Let's watch."

"Everything takes so long to grow," grumbled Jamey. "Backyard gardens are boring."

"Not if we're time detectives," suggested their mother. "Then we can make some exciting discoveries."

4

"How can we do that?" asked Jamey.

"Well, let's look at this old leaf, which fell from the tree last autumn. How do you think the tree got here?"

"I know!" said Megan. "Daddy told me a story about our oak tree. Long ago, a squirrel buried an acorn to eat later. When the squirrel forgot to dig it up, the acorn sprouted. And that might be how this big tree began to grow."

"Do you see that dip in the ground that runs through all our neighbors' backyards?" asked Mother. "A hundred years ago, before there were houses here, it was a creek."

"That means fish swam here, and animals came to drink. I can almost see them," Jamey said excitedly.

"I can go back farther than that," said Father. "I just dug up this big rock. Where do you think it came from?"

"Wasn't it always here?"

"No. Millions of years ago, even before there were people on the planet, lava flowed from volcanoes. It cooled and hardened into this rock. Then, during one of the Ice Ages, a glacier dragged it and other huge boulders over long distances. When the ice melted, the rocks were left behind."

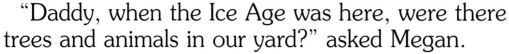

"Daddy, when the Ice Age was here, were there trees and animals in our yard?" asked Megan.

"No. It was too cold for them. Our yard was buried under ice far deeper than the tallest buildings."

"Wow!" exclaimed Jamey. "Backyard detective work is more exciting than I thought."

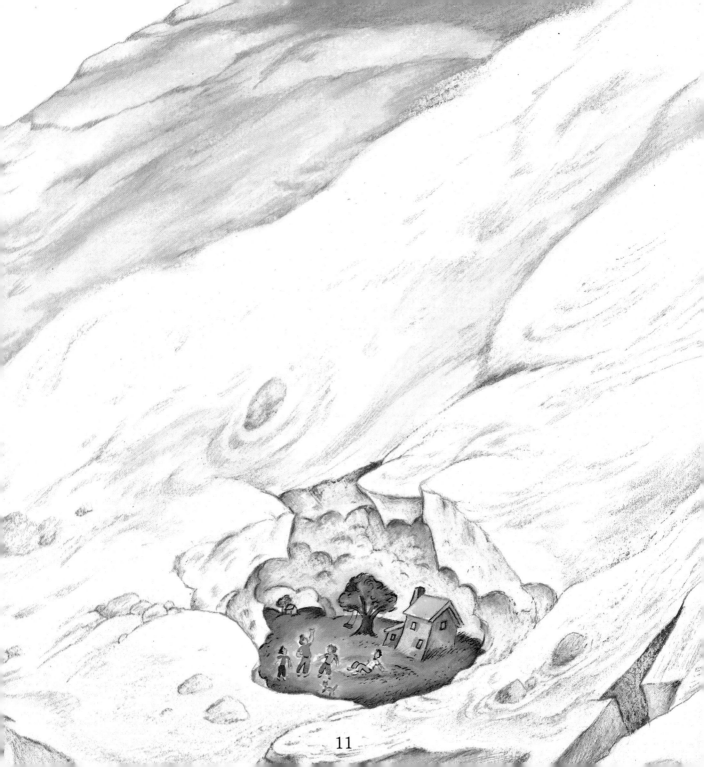

"Here are some more clues to the past."

"All I see is dirt," said Megan.

"Look closer," said Mother. "Some of the dirt is made of tiny grains of sand, and most of it is dark and thick with twigs and leaves. Each of those things comes from a different time."

"The grains of sand are all that's left of rocks that got worn down," explained Father. "The twigs and leaves are much newer. Even the vegetable scraps from last night's dinner will become part of the soil. It takes time for them to break down, though."

"Look at this weird nail," cried Jamey. "It has square sides and rust all over it."

"Good hunting, Jamey! That nail is a real find," said Mother. "It's probably more than a hundred years old. Early settlers who cleared this land might have used it to build a house right here."

14

"My friend Jenny found this arrowhead down where the creek used to be," said Megan.

"The Native people who lived here shaped arrowheads out of stones," Father explained. "They likely used them for hunting the animals that lived by the water."

"Can time detectives look into the future?" asked Megan.

"Of course," said Father. "Look at these seeds. Later this summer we'll eat the vegetables that grow from them. The fruit tree at the bottom of the garden has blossoms now. In the fall we'll be able to pick apples."

"Look!" shouted Jamey. "There's a robin building a nest. In a few weeks there'll be baby birds in our yard."

"Right," added Father. "And look up in the oak tree. There's a squirrel's nest. Our backyard could have lots of babies in it this summer."

21

"What about hundreds of years from now? What will our yard look like then?"

"To figure that out we have to use our imaginations," said Mother. "Maybe the city will get bigger, and there'll be highways and skyscrapers everywhere."

"Or perhaps the plants and animals will take over our house and yard," suggested Father.

"What if pollution takes over?" asked Jamey.

"Yes," said Father, "that could happen if we're not careful."

"Then let's be careful," said Jamey. "Let's make gardens instead of garbage."

"I like that idea," agreed Father.

"What about time detectives of the future?" asked Megan. "I want to leave something for them in this backyard."

"Me, too!" yelled Jamey. "Could we put something about us in a tin box and bury it in the garden?"

"That's a great idea! But let's use this glass jar instead. It won't rust away, and it could even be a clue for those future investigators. Let's all put something in it."

"I have a coin in my pocket," offered Jamey.

"I'm putting in my marble and the ring from Jenny's party," said Megan.

"And I'll take a story out of today's newspaper," added Mother.

"Wait for me! I'll be back in a minute." Father rushed into the house.

In no time he was back.

"It's a picture of us all," he said.

On the bottom he wrote,
The Backyard Time Detectives.

Be a Time Detective

Go back through the pages of this book. Can you find more clues for the time detectives? Here are some hints to help you:

On *page 3* there is a caterpillar on Father's hand. What do you think it will become? Look at the other pages. Can you find it?

On *pages 4 and 5* seeds are being carried by animals to new locations. Can you find burrs on the dog and a sunflower seed being dropped by the chickadee?

On *pages 8 and 9* you can see into the past when the volcanoes erupted and rocks were formed. Under the crust of the earth, hot, liquid rock still flows. It sometimes erupts in volcanoes.

On *pages 10 and 11* you can see some of the enormous glaciers that once covered much of North America. The ice was so massive that it pushed anything in its path, even mountains. Did glaciers cover the place where *you* live?

On *pages 12 and 13* are some of the ways soil is made. Soil is formed when once-living things decay. If there was no decay, remains of dead plants and animals would pile up everywhere. Many animals, including woodpeckers and insects, break dead plants into smaller pieces. Fungi and bacteria break them down even more. Earthworms are excellent soil makers. They eat the earth and digest it, passing many tons of it through their bodies each year.

On *pages 16 and 17* are people who lived here even longer ago. In those days, Native people of North America used the plants and animals around them to provide everything they needed. What could *you* use to build a house if there were no stores to go to?

On *pages 18 and 19* are the seeds and the plants they will become later in the summer. The blossoms on the apple tree will turn into fruit.

On *pages 20 and 21* are the babies that will be born or hatch this spring and summer. Some parents, like the robins and squirrels, take care of their young. Others, like the turtle, leave their eggs behind. Their babies must fend for themselves. Did you know that all the paper wasps in the nest have the same mother? Only the queen wasp lays eggs, and she may have hundreds of children.

On *pages 22 and 23* the city has spread over Megan and Jamey's backyard. What has happened to the plants and animals?

On *pages 26 and 27* are two different ways the future might look. Which would you choose? What can you do to help it come true?

Why not leave some clues for future time detectives in your area? Ask a grownup to help you put together a time capsule. Maybe ten, fifty, or hundreds of years from now, someone will find it.